Franklin Delano Roosevelt
(1882–1945)

QUOTATIONS
OF
Franklin
Delano
Roosevelt

APPLEWOOD BOOKS
Carlisle, Massachusetts

Franklin Delano Roosevelt

FRANKLIN DELANO ROOSEVELT was born January 30, 1882 on his family's estate on the Hudson River in Hyde Park, New York. He graduated from Harvard University in 1904 and went on to study law at Columbia University. In 1905, he married Eleanor Roosevelt, who was his fifth cousin and the adored niece of then-President Theodore Roosevelt.

FDR idolized his "cousin Theodore" and followed his path into politics. FDR was elected to the New York State Senate in 1910 and in 1913, was appointed Assistant Secretary of the Navy by President Woodrow Wilson. He ran unsuccessfully for Vice President in 1920 on the Democratic ticket with James Cox. In 1921, a devastating polio attack left him paralyzed. His promising political career seemed doomed.

Roosevelt struggled against great odds to regain the strength in his legs, but was never able to walk again. With the help of Eleanor Roosevelt, who kept his name alive in New York politics, FDR was elected Governor in 1928. He was nominated for the presidency in 1932, and, with the nation deep in the Great Depression, defeated President Herbert Hoover.

FDR's "New Deal" put people back to work, insured bank deposits, regulated the stock market, saved homes and farms, and created Social Security. The Civilian Conservation Corps, Tennessee Valley Authority, Works Progress Administration, and the Public Works Administration created a legacy of public buildings, parks, art, and infrastructure projects that enriched American life. FDR was reelected in 1936 by the largest landslide in American history, creating the New Deal coalition (labor unions, minorities, liberal farm groups, intellectuals, and the white South) that dominated American politics for the next thirty years.

Halfway through his second term, Roosevelt began to plan for his retirement, which he planned to devote to working with his vast collection of books, ship models, art, family memorabilia and organizing his papers from more than 25 years in public office. No single institution would accept the entire collection, so FDR raised money privately to build the Roosevelt Library on his estate in Hyde Park. The only presidential library used by a sitting president, it is the first in our system of presidential libraries, part of the National Archives.

As the world erupted in war in 1939, the United States maintained a longstanding neutrality. In 1940, Roosevelt was elected to an unprecedented Third Term and immediately enacted Lend-Lease, making the U.S. the "arsenal of democracy," providing aid to Britain and eventually the Soviet Union. The first peace-time draft was enacted and the army and navy were dramatically strengthened.

After the Pearl Harbor attack on December 7, 1941, FDR mobilized the nation to fight in both Europe and the Pacific. With Winston Churchill and Josef Stalin, FDR led the "Big Three" and their Allies to the unconditional defeat of the Axis powers. His vision for the United Nations led to the creation of the first permanent international peace-making organization.

Reelected to an unprecedented Fourth Term in 1944, Franklin Roosevelt died in Warm Springs, Georgia on April 12, 1945. Widely hailed as the friend of the "common man," critics in recent years have criticized war-time policies on Japanese-American internment and the Holocaust.

QUOTATIONS
OF
Franklin Delano Roosevelt

The country needs and, unless I mistake its temper, the country demands bold persistent experimentation. It is common sense to take a method and try it. If it fails, admit it frankly and try another. But above all, try something.

Address at Oglethorpe University, Atlanta, Georgia, 5/22/1932

Franklin D. Roosevelt

Happiness lies not in the mere possession of money; it lies in the joy of achievement, in the thrill of creative effort.

First Inaugural Address, 3/4/1933

This great Nation will endure as it has
endured, will revive and will prosper. So,
first of all, let me assert my firm belief that
the only thing we have to fear is fear
itself—nameless, unreasoning, unjustified
terror which paralyzes needed efforts to
convert retreat into advance.

First Inaugural Address, 3/4/1933

Franklin D Roosevelt

We think of our land and water and
human resources not as static and sterile
possessions but as life-giving assets to be
administered by wise provision for future
days.

*Message to Congress on the Use of Our
National Resources, 1/24/1935*

*H*istory is filled with unforeseeable situations that call for some flexibility of action.

Statement on Neutrality Legislation, 8/31/1935

Franklin D. Roosevelt

*D*emocracy is not a static thing. It is an everlasting march.

Address at Los Angeles, Calif., 10/1/1935

Franklin D. Roosevelt

*T*he history of every Nation is eventually written in the way in which it cares for its soil.

Statement on Signing the Soil Conservation and Domestic Allotment Act, 3/1/1936

$\mathcal{T}$here is a mysterious cycle in human events. To some generations much is given. Of other generations much is expected. This generation of Americans has a rendezvous with destiny.

Acceptance Speech for the Renomination for the Presidency, Philadelphia, Pa., 6/27/1936

Franklin D. Roosevelt

$\mathcal{B}$etter the occasional faults of a Government that lives in a spirit of charity than the consistent omissions of a Government frozen in the ice of its own indifference.

Acceptance Speech for the Renomination for the Presidency, Philadelphia, Pa., 6/27/1936

*L*iberty requires opportunity to make a living—a living decent according to the standard of the time, a living which gives man not only enough to live by, but something to live for.

Acceptance Speech for the Renomination for the Presidency, Philadelphia, Pa., 6/27/1936

*... T*here is nothing in Nature I am as fond of as a tree.

Remarks at Asheville, N.C., 9/10/1936

*T*he school is the last expenditure upon which America should be willing to economize.

Campaign Address, Kansas City, Mo., 10/13/1936

*H*ere is my principle: Taxes shall be levied according to ability to pay. That is the only American principle.

Address at Worcester, Mass., 10/21/1936

Franklin D. Roosevelt

*L*iberty and peace are living things. In each generation—if they are to be maintained—they must be guarded and vitalized anew.

Address on the Occasion of the Fiftieth Anniversary of the Statue of Liberty, 10/28/1936

Franklin D. Roosevelt

*I*n our personal ambitions we are individualists. But in our seeking for economic and political progress as a nation, we all go up, or else we all go down, as one people.

Second Inaugural Address, 1/20/1937

*T*he test of our progress is not whether we add more to the abundance of those who have much; it is whether we provide enough for those who have too little.

Second Inaugural Address, 1/20/1937

Franklin D. Roosevelt

*T*he Constitution of the United States was a layman's document, not a lawyer's contract. That cannot be stressed too often.

Address on Constitution Day,
Washington, D.C., 9/17/1937

Franklin D. Roosevelt

I never forget that I live in a house owned by all the American people and that I have been given their trust.

Fireside Chat, 4/14/1938

*T*he only real capital of a nation is its natural resources and its human beings. So long as we take care of and make the most of both of them, we shall survive as a strong nation, a successful nation and a progressive nation.

Address before the National Education Association,
New York City, 6/30/1938

Franklin D. Roosevelt

*L*et us not be afraid to help each other—let us never forget that government is ourselves and not an alien power over us. The ultimate rulers of our democracy are not a President and Senators and Congressmen and Government officials but the voters of this country.

Address at the Dedication of a Memorial to
the Northwest Territory, Marietta, Ohio, 7/8/1938

*D*emocracy cannot succeed unless those who express their choice are prepared to choose wisely. The real safeguard of democracy, therefore, is education.

Message for American Education Week,
9/27/1938

Franklin D Roosevelt

*T*he greatest single resource of this country is its youth, and no progressive Government can afford to ignore the needs of its future citizens for adequate schooling and for that useful work which establishes them as a part of its economy.

Message to Congress Requesting Relief
Appropriations, 4/27/1939

*T*he arts cannot thrive except where men are free to be themselves and to be in charge of the discipline of their own energies and ardors.

Radio Dedication of the Museum of Modern Art, New York City, 5/10/1939

Franklin D. Roosevelt

A Radical is a man with both feet firmly planted—in the air.

A Conservative is a man with two perfectly good legs who, however, has never learned to walk forward.

A Reactionary is a somnambulist walking backwards.

A Liberal is a man who uses his legs and his hands at the behest—at the command—of his head.

Radio Address to the New York Herald Tribune Forum, 10/26/1939

Repetition does not transform a lie into a truth.

> *Radio Address to the New York Herald*
> *Tribune Forum, 10/26/1939*

Franklin D. Roosevelt

It is one of the characteristics of a free and democratic modern nation that it have free and independent labor unions.

> *Address at Teamsters Union Convention,*
> *Washington, D.C., 9/11/1940*

Franklin D. Roosevelt

Wherever men and women of good will gather together to serve their community, there is America.

> *Radio Address for the Mobilization*
> *for Human Needs, 10/13/1940*

*H*uman kindness has never weakened
the stamina or softened the fiber of a free
people. A nation does not have to be cruel
in order to be tough.

*Radio Address for the Mobilization
for Human Needs, 10/13/1940*

I consider it a public duty to answer
falsifications with facts. I will not pretend
that I find this an unpleasant duty. I am an
old campaigner, and I love a good fight.

*Campaign Address
at Philadelphia, Pa., 10/23/1940*

We are telling the world that we are free—
and we intend to remain free and at peace.
We are free to live and love and laugh.
We face the future with confidence and
courage. We are American.

Campaign Address at Boston, Mass., 10/30/1940

Franklin D Roosevelt

Whoever seeks to set one religion
against another seeks to destroy all religion.

Campaign Address, Brooklyn, N.Y., 11/1/1940

Franklin D Roosevelt

It is an unfortunate human failing that a
full pocketbook often groans more loudly
than an empty stomach.

Campaign Address, Brooklyn, N.Y., 11/1/1940

*A*lways the heart and the soul of our country will be the heart and the soul of the common man—the men and the women who never have ceased to believe in democracy, who never have ceased to love their families, their homes, and their country.

Campaign Address, Cleveland, Ohio, 11/2/1940

Franklin D. Roosevelt

I see an America whose rivers and valleys and lakes—hills and streams and plains— the mountains over our land and nature's wealth deep under the earth—are protected as the rightful heritage of all the people.

Campaign Address, Cleveland, Ohio, 11/2/1940

We have more faith in the collective opinion of all Americans than in the individual opinion of any one American.

> *Radio Campaign Address,*
> *Hyde Park, N.Y., 11/4/1940*

Franklin D. Roosevelt

We must be the great arsenal of democracy.

> *Fireside Chat, White House,*
> *Washington, D.C., 12/29/1940*

Franklin D. Roosevelt

In the future days, which we seek to make secure, we look forward to a world founded upon four essential human freedoms.

The first is freedom of speech and expression—everywhere in the world.

The second is freedom of every person to

worship God in his own way—everywhere in the world.

The third is freedom from want—which, translated into world terms, means economic understandings which will secure to every nation a healthy peacetime life for its inhabitants—everywhere in the world.

The fourth is freedom from fear—which, translated into world terms, means a world-wide reduction of armaments to such a point and in such a thorough fashion that no nation will be in a position to commit an act of physical aggression against any neighbor—anywhere in the world.

Annual Message to Congress, 1/6/1941

A Nation, like a person, has a mind—a mind that must be kept informed and alert, that must know itself, that understands the hopes and the needs of its neighbors—all the other Nations that live within the narrowing circle of the world.

Third Inaugural Address, 1/20/1941

Franklin D. Roosevelt

*T*he democratic aspiration is no mere recent phase in human history. It is human history. It permeated the ancient life of early peoples. It blazed anew in the Middle Ages. It was written in Magna Carta.

Third Inaugural Address, 1/20/1941

$\mathcal{D}$ictators—those who enforce the totalitarian form of government—think it a dangerous thing for their unfortunate peoples to know that in our democracy officers of the Government are the servants, and never the masters of the people.

Address to the Academy Awards Dinner,
2/27/1941

Franklin D. Roosevelt

$\mathcal{N}$o nation combating the increasing threat of totalitarianism can afford arbitrarily to exclude large segments of its population from its defense industries. Even more important is it for us to strengthen our unity and morale by refuting at home the very theories which we are fighting abroad.

Memorandum Condemning Discrimination in
Defense Work, 6/12/1941

I assume that the German leaders are not deeply concerned, tonight or any other time, by what we Americans or the American Government say or publish about them. We cannot bring about the downfall of Nazi-ism by the use of long-range invective. But when you see a rattlesnake poised to strike, you do not wait until he has struck before you crush him.

Fireside Chat, 9/11/1941

Y esterday, December 7, 1941—a date which will live in infamy—the United States of America was suddenly and deliberately attacked by naval and air forces of the Empire of Japan.

Address to Congress Requesting a Declaration of War with Japan, 12/8/1941

*N*o matter how long it may take us to overcome this premeditated invasion, the American people in their righteous might will win through to absolute victory.

Address to Congress Requesting a Declaration of War with Japan, 12/8/1941

Franklin D Roosevelt

*Y*ou know I am a juggler, and I never let my right hand know what my left hand does.

Quoting Himself in a Memorandum of a Conversation with Morgenthau, Presidential Diary, Morgenthau Papers, 5/15/1942

*T*he four freedoms of common humanity
are as much elements of man's needs as air
and sunlight, bread and salt. Deprive him
of all these freedoms and he dies—deprive
him of a part of them and a part of him
withers. Give them to him in full and
abundant measure and he will cross the
threshold of a new age, the greatest age of
man.

Radio Address on United Flag Day, 6/14/1942

A nation of home owners, of people
who own a real share in their own land, is
unconquerable.

*Letter to United States Savings and Loan
League War Conference, Chicago, Ill.,
11/10/1942*

We have supreme confidence that, with the help of God, honor will prevail. We have faith that future generations will know that here, in the middle of the twentieth century, there came a time when men of good will found a way to unite, and produce, and fight to destroy the forces of ignorance, and intolerance, and slavery, and war.

Address to the White House Correspondents'
Association, 2/12/1943

Franklin D. Roosevelt

All that is within me cries out to go back to my home on the Hudson River, to avoid public responsibilities, and to avoid also the publicity which in our democracy follows every step of the Nation's Chief Executive.

Letter Agreeing to Accept a Nomination for a
Fourth Term, 7/11/1944

*N*obody will ever deprive the American people of the right to vote except the American people themselves—and the only way they could do that is by not voting at all.

Radio Address from the White House, 10/5/1944

Franklin D. Roosevelt

*T*he American people have a good habit —the habit of going right ahead and accomplishing the impossible.

Address at Soldiers Field, Chicago, Ill.,
10/28/1944

W e seek peace—enduring peace. More than an end to war, we want an end to the beginnings of all wars—yes, an end to this brutal, inhuman, and thoroughly impractical method of settling the differences between governments.

Undelivered Address Prepared for Jefferson Day,
4/13/1945

Franklin D. Roosevelt

T he only limit to our realization of tomorrow will be our doubts of today. Let us move forward with strong and active faith.

Undelivered Address Prepared for Jefferson Day,
4/13/1945